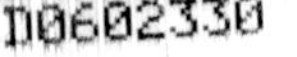

This is the Dog

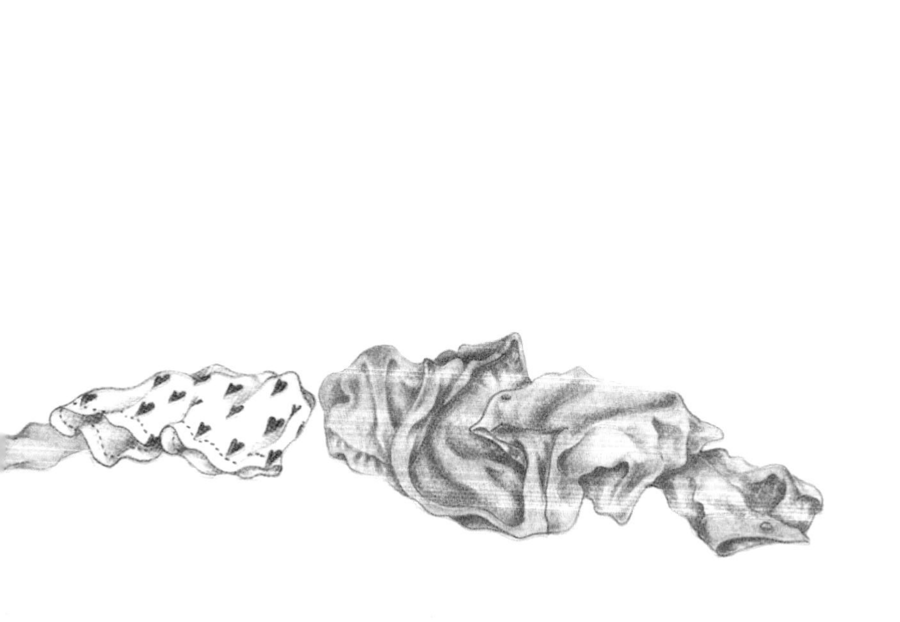

To Ali, Cloe, and Katie, my three dog-loving daughters

– Sheryl

For my three girls, Adria, Jade and Julia

– Chrissie

Published in Canada by Fitzhenry & Whiteside,
195 Allstate Parkway, Markham, Ontario L3R 4T8

Published in the United States by Fitzhenry & Whiteside,
121 Harvard Avenue, Suite 2, Allston, Massachusetts 02134

www.fitzhenry.ca godwit@fitzhenry.ca

10 9 8 7 6 5 4 3 2 1

National Library of Canada Cataloguing in Publication
McFarlane, Sheryl, 1954-
This is the dog / by Sheryl McFarlane ; illustrated by Chrissie Wysotti
ISBN 1-55041-551-4 (bound).--ISBN 1-55041-806-8 (pbk.)
1. Puppies--Juvenile fiction. 2. Dogs--Juvenile fiction. I. Wysotti, Chrissie II. Title.
PS8575.F39T46 2003 jC813'.54 C2002-905304-8
PZ7

U.S. Publisher Cataloging-in-Publication Data
(Library of Congress Standards)

McFarlane, Sheryl.
This is the dog / by Sheryl McFarlane ; illustrated by Chrissie Wysotti.--1st ed.
[32] p. : col. ill. ; cm.
Summary: The puppy has escaped in this rhyming picture book.
Chaos erupts everywhere he goes throughout the town.
ISBN 1-55041-551-4
ISBN 1-55041-806-8 (pbk.)
1. Dogs-- Fiction. I. Wysotti, Chrissie. II. Title.
[E] 21 PZ7.M34.T5 2003

Fitzhenry & Whiteside acknowledges with thanks the Canada Council for the Arts, the Government of Canada through the Book Publishing Industry Development Program (BPIDP), and the Ontario Arts Council for their support for our publishing program.

Design by Wycliffe Smith Design

Printed in Hong Kong

This is the Dog

BY SHERYL MCFARLANE

illustrated by Chrissie Wysotski

Fitzhenry & Whiteside

This is the dog
too excited to stay,
a tail-wagging puppy
all ready to play.

This is his owner
spunky and quick,
too busy for dress-up
or fetching a stick.

This is the stall
where the pup took a shine
to hot dogs so yummy
and ice cream divine.

295

This is the family
not happy to share
cookies and juice
with a bundle of hair.

This is the fisherman
caught by surprise
by a four-legged thief
who pounced on his prize.

These are the seagulls
that stirred up the chase,
snatching the fish
from the pup's hiding place.

This is the teacher
throwing a fit,
his papers all splattered
with crumbs, drool, and grit.

Aa Bb Cc
Dd Ee Ff

These are the teens
hanging out at the beach
that cheered on the hound
and his high-flying reach.

This is the castle,
almost complete,
caught in the path
of four over-sized feet.

This is the tomcat
that no dog should chase,
not if he valued the nose
on his face.

This is the puppy
without any pride,
licking his wounds
and hitching a ride.

This is the mother
they tried to sneak past,
muddy and grubby,
together at last.

This is the welcome
that waited at home:
a bath…

fluffy towels…

cookies…

a bone.